THIS BOOK BELONGS TO

....

....

HEY DUGGEE

LADYBIRD BOOKS

UK | USA | Canada | Ireland | Australia | India | New Zealand | South Africa

Ladybird Books is part of the Penguin Random House group of companies
whose addresses can be found at global.penguinrandomhouse.com.

www.penguin.co.uk   www.puffin.co.uk   www.ladybird.co.uk

**Penguin
Random House
UK**

First published 2023
001

Text and illustrations copyright © Studio AKA Limited, 2023
Adapted by Mandy Archer, based on "The Sailing Badge" written by Sam Morrison

Printed in China

The authorized representative in the EEA is Penguin Random House Ireland,
Morrison Chambers, 32 Nassau Street, Dublin D02 YH68

A CIP catalogue record for this book is available from the British Library

ISBN: 978-1-405-95375-7

All correspondence to:
Ladybird Books, Penguin Random House Children's
One Embassy Gardens, 8 Viaduct Gardens, London SW11 7BW

DUGGEE

DUGGEE
AND THE
PIRATES

TAG   NORRIE   HAPPY   ROLY   BETTY

Duggee and the Squirrels are enjoying a fun day at the beach.

Duggee is relaxing on a deckchair, and the Squirrels are building sandcastles. How lovely!

Suddenly, an enormous ship slides on to the sand.
The Squirrels gasp. What a funny place to park!

Duggee and the Squirrels climb aboard the ship. It seems to be empty.

Then, when Betty opens a door . . .

five penguins and a parrot roll out!

One of the penguins steps forward.
"I'm Captain Red Moustache,
and this is my crew," he says.

Captain Red Moustache and his crew are all sick. They have
eaten too much fish ice cream!

"We were supposed to be heading to this island to pick something up," he says, "but now we're too poorly to sail."

Duggee and the Squirrels offer to sail the penguins' ship to the island. Duggee knows all about sailing. He has his **Sailing Badge!**

First, the Squirrels get to know the ship.

Suddenly, Happy spots something sailing towards them. It's a fishing boat!

HELLO!

ABOUT-TURN!

The fishing boat turns round quickly and chugs away.

In fact, NO ONE seems very pleased to see the ship.

Not the octopus . . .

the shark . . .

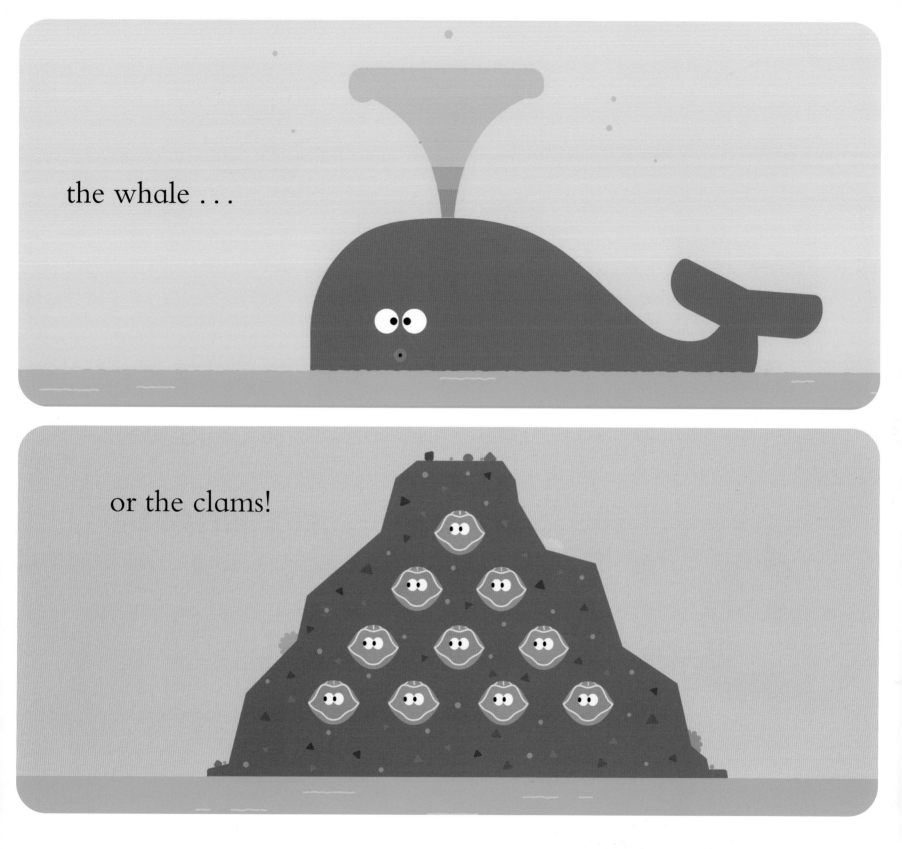

the whale . . .

or the clams!

How strange . . .

Soon, the ship arrives at the island and everybody gets off.
"Oh, good," says Captain Red Moustache, looking at his map.
"This is definitely where we left it."

LEFT WHAT?

"Erm, our medicine!" replies Captain Red Moustache.
"It is going to make us feel much better."

Roly helps the penguins dig up a big, heavy box.

But there isn't any medicine inside . . .

The Squirrels think about the penguins' clothes, the parrot and everyone running away. Now everything makes sense.

"All right. We ARE pirates," admits the captain.
"And we stole this treasure!"

BECAUSE THAT'S WHAT PIRATES DO!

The Squirrels tell the pirates to give all the treasure back.

BECAUSE THAT'S WHAT SQUIRRELS DO!

The Squirrels raise a new flag on the ship. It's time to go sailing again to return all the treasure. First, they find the fishing boat.

"Go on," says Betty.
"Sorry we stole your goldfish, Captain Fisherman!" says
Captain Red Moustache.

"Sorry, Octopus!"

"Sorry, Shark!"

"Sorry, Whale!"

"Sorry, Clams!"

Everyone is very happy to get their treasure back.
The voyage is over. The pirates drop the Squirrels back to shore.

"I hope you pirates have learned your lesson," says Norrie.

"We have." Captain Red Moustache sighs. "No more fish ice cream . . . and no more stealing!"

GOODBYE!

The pirates wave goodbye to the Squirrels.

Haven't the Squirrels done well today, Duggee?

AH-WOOF!

They have definitely earned their **Sailing Badges**.

Now there's just time for one last thing before the
Squirrels go home . . .

"DUGGEE HUG!"